Heroine Chic

James William Purcell Webster

Dear Alex,

FACE!*

[signature]

Inspired
Quill

* Ok, fine, I'll pony up and write
something: you're great. You absurd anime protagonist,
you.

Published by Inspired Quill: September 2017

First Edition

Contact the author through their website:
strangelittlestories.tumblr.com

Chief Editor: Sara-Jayne Slack
Cover Design: Venetia Jackson
Typeset in Minion Pro

Paperback ISBN: 978-1-908600-65-3
eBook ISBN: 978-1-908600-66-0
Print Edition

Printed in the United Kingdom
1 2 3 4 5 6 7 8 9 10

Inspired Quill Publishing, UK
Business Reg. No. 7592847
www.inspired-quill.com

To all the heroines who inspire me so often.
To those who soar on scales. To those who writhe in the deep.
I hope I have done justice to the wonder of your stories.

Table of Contents

Long Ago

It was in the Long Ago
that we first dug our nails
into sharp dirt
when the frosts bit the air
and us
the earth starved
and the growing shadows
the deepening dark
gathered up and swelled to stalk us
cackling
growing their shadow teeth
learning to lick their shadow lips
in the Early Days when we were young and I was weak
and the cold and shadows clawed and sucked my flesh
'til I was barely there
skin taut over the drum of my chest
legs more ache and hope than muscled sure-steps
leaning on you

feet stumbling and eyes dimming
slowly filling with shadows
and you cut off your hair
and wove it into a whip
and the air streaked with gold
as you made sparks crack between frost
and you took one of my ribs
ripped it from the cave of my chest with bloodied grasping
    nails
sharpened it to a point with your teeth
it did for a knife
that made the shadows bleed.
You licked the wound that was my rib
flicked your tongue into the gap and tasted the life of me
and lapped at me 'til the pain faded
'til your hunger sated
and you opened me up
put me in the earth
and it hungered no more
the grey dirt turned brown
thawed by me
and the sparks of your hair warmed the air into the first
    summer
and the plants of the world grew out of my chest
and you walked
bloody
hunting in amongst the forests of my body
and people wondered

later

when we were ages old

why you sometimes kissed the trees.

The Only Little Girl in the World

ONCE UPON A time, there was a little girl who lived alone in a forest, for she was the only little girl in all the world.

Where were this girl's parents? Well, as they are not important to this story, it's probably safe to assume they're dead or evil or cursed or something.

Now, the forest in which the girl lived was dark and cold and full of monsters, so the little girl built a house out of logs and she was snug and safe inside it.

Shortly after she had finished it, there was a knock on the door. *Who could be knocking?* she thought. *No-one even knows I live here yet.*

And when she opened the door, all the monsters of the forest were crowded around outside in a sea of claws and eyes and undulous limbs.

Please little girl, said the monsters, *it's very cold and scary out here. Could we come in?*

Alright, said the little girl, *so long as you promise to* behave.

We promise.

So the little girl let them in on the proviso they'd be on their very best behaviour.

And while they did behave, it was awfully cramped with all those monsters in the girl's house, like a game of sardines where everyone's mostly made of teeth. And the little girl wasn't very comfortable, so she went outside into the woods.

The woods were still very cold and very dark and for a while the little girl was tempted to set it on fire; but while that would solve the problem, she felt like it would cause a few problems of its own so she didn't do that.

Instead, the little girl took a few shiny stones from the earth, and she asked them very nicely if they wouldn't mind sitting up in the sky for a while and sprinkling a few sparkles down on the forest.

They thought the girl was very sweet, so they agreed it was a capital idea and she threw them as hard as she could and up they went. They glitter there still.

As it was still cold, the girl went and spoke to the dragon of the forest, who was so big and so old that they weren't afraid of anything.

And the little girl asked if maybe sometimes the dragon wouldn't mind breathing some fire and keeping things warm.

The dragon didn't really see what was in it for them…

So the girl pointed out the shiny stones she'd set in the

sky and said, *Dragon, if you give me just a bit of fire every day then they shall all be yours.*

And the dragon said, *They seem awfully far away.*

But she had her answer ready: *You have wings, dragon, you could fly up there and spread your wings across the whole sky and they could be your hoard.*

The dragon liked the sound of this very much, so from then on they agreed to light up the sky with warm fire for half of every day. And that's just what they did.

Feeling thoroughly satisfied, the girl went back to her house…

Where she was promptly eaten by the monsters, as she had been away so long they'd quite forgotten their promise to behave.

And all the little bits of the girl in the monsters' tummies were furious. She had charmed the stars. She knew the secret of the dragon who became the sun. And she was displeased.

So she began to twist and turn and change the monsters from within and they all suffered the most terrible stomach aches that had them rolling on the floor in pain.

And when they got up, they weren't monsters any more, but humans.

They spread out through the forest and began making houses and tools and bargains with other monsters in the lands beyond.

But, deep down, there would always be a little bit of

monster left behind.

This is why most people can be quite unpleasant.

But even further down, is a little piece of the little girl who lived alone in the wood.

This is why most people are quite extraordinary.

Morning After

SHE WOKE WITH a pounding head and no memory of the night before.

Looking at the crater around her, the detritus of the cracked city still settling like snow, she came to the obvious conclusion.

"Must've been a cracking night."

She curled up in her blanket of debris to catch up on her sleep.

And her dreams were all explosions.

Manic Pixie Nightmare Girl

H E WASN'T SURE where she came from; she'd first shown up during an eclipse at the exact moment the moon swallowed the sun, smelling of ozone and regret.

They'd had coffee. She told the barista her name was Lil and he misspelt it as "The Adversary" and she'd laughed so loud half the staff fainted. Halfway through the coffee date he noticed she had blood on her face.

"You're bleeding," he said.

"It happens," she said.

The next time, she appeared during a thunderstorm and they had spiced tea on an abandoned rooftop café. It tasted like gems cut with fireworks, exploding on his tongue. As they sipped their tea she told him a story about a dance of ghosts and foxes that left him stunned. When he came to, she was gone.

Over the next few years, she came and went as she pleased. Once he tried to get her number, but she just cackled and when he next unlocked his phone the glass was cracked in the shape of a summoning glyph. For the most part it was ruined, except for the occasional pictures of lions, lynxes and leering dragons she would text him captioned with the word "KITTY!"

The second to last time he saw her was in the midst of a meteor shower. As rocks fell from the great vacuum of the sky and flowered into conflagrations on the city below, she popped out from behind a shadow.

"I have a free moment between odd jobs," she said absent-mindedly. "I could take you out for sushi if you'd like?"

He did like and they exchanged witticisms over rice and vegetables amongst the flickering shadows, flames and debris.

The last time he saw her was beneath a forest of tall towers made of gleaming jet. Their jagged points dripped with dark ichor from where they pierced the sky.

"You're bleeding again," he said.

"No," she said. "I'm not."

You couldn't call what she did next a smile, but there were definitely teeth involved.

The Girl With The Candle In Her Heart

THERE ONCE WAS a girl with a candle in her heart.

And every day, when she got up, she would see the world was dark and cold and strike a piece of steel against her flinty chest (for she always kept her tinder box nearby). And her heart would splutter into bright, warm light, which lit up her little corner of the darkness.

In the course of her day, the candle would usually flutter and fade as various people jostled her. She lived in a very busy city, which made it very easy to see those around you as obstacles instead of people. So not many noticed the light of her little candle, and they would bump her and spill some of the wax from her chest onto the ground.

Other times, a great dark tide would descend on the city. Many were able to ignore it, for they were very busy people and could only deal with so much in a day, and they would row through its murky waters on rafts made out of "not my problems" and "oh that is very far aways" and "isn't that terribles". Sometimes, the girl was able to do this too. But other times, the shadowy waves would buffet her harshly and she would fall to the ground, weeping hot, tallow tears. On those days, you could tell where the girl had been by following the trail of dried wax.

But most often, the girl's candle ran low because whenever she saw someone whose own chest had gone dark, she would press hers to theirs and let the flame of her candle catch the wick of their heart.

Sometimes these were people who had been jostled too many times. Others were those who, if they did not find their way, were at risk of being pulled beneath the inky depths. Sometimes their hearts had gone dark for no reason at all.

But whatever the cause, the girl gave them a little bit of her flame. Even though the act of doing so caused more wax to spill and sometimes made her world seem a very dark place indeed.

One day, when the girl's own candle had dripped down to its stub, she realised she did not even have enough light to see outside her own house. So she spent the day inside, trying to scrape together enough tallow to bolster her meagre flame.

Then there was a knock at the door.

Standing outside were the people whose candles the girl had re-lit.

There were a great many of them.

"We just wanted to thank you," they said together, smiling little embarrassed smiles. "For you have made us so warm and happy over the years."

The girl felt an inferno flickering to life in her chest.

"So we got you this…"

From behind the crowd walked a strange, misshapen figure. It was made entirely of candle wax and a long, thick wick ran all the way through its body. Where it should have had a head, it instead had a candle flame that burned ever so bright. It was very handsome in its way.

"You see, every time you gave a little bit of your fire to us, we each fell a little bit in love with you. And, seeing as you were so dear to us, we scooped up the wax that you spilt and clung to it like a treasure."

They smiled at each other, all bathed in the glow of the girl and the golem made of wax.

"And then, when the time came that we had warmth to spare, we gathered up all the pieces of you that we had, as well as all those we could find that other people knocked from you, and we put them all together. And then we kissed the air until our lips struck sparks in the wind and that wind lit the wick. And then the candle came to life."

The construction they had made took several more shy steps forwards, until it stood next to the girl and, between the two of them, it was like every inch of her skin were glowing. It took her hand and both their hands were warm.

"This is the light that you put out into the world."

The golem's flame flared for a second, as if it were smiling.

"And now it is coming back to you."

Riddle Me This

THE EMPEROR-GENERAL'S CRUSADE had just reached its fourth year, and so far it had been a stirring success; almost all the monsters had been rooted out from under beds, djinn were ejected from their lamps, and the fairies who fed on teeth had been lured out with choice molars and captured for training.

Now the crusade had moved on from dealing with domestic threats and began to turn its attention outwards to the lawless fairytale wastelands, a perilous place where passing traders were terrorised by big bad wolves and where every old woman was (not-so) secretly a wicked witch.

"It's not a question of us versus them," the Emperor-General told his detractors (for he encouraged and prized rational debate). "It's not about mortal versus fable. Fact versus fiction. It's a simple question of modernisation. The supernatural *must* adapt to the times or be left behind."

By now, having already burnt a path through the deep,

dark forest to make way for new roads, the advancing troops had begun to sweep through the various towns and villages. The inhabiting fairies, nymphs and genus loci fled before them.

The ranking officer, one Major Hansel, had chased a particularly troublesome bunch of spirits back to a local school. Loath as they were to disrupt a place of learning, he and his men all agreed that they could not allow the spirits to lurk around such impressionable young minds.

That's when they encountered the sphinx.

She stood at the school's entrance, her body formed of bright red brick, her beak of sharp blackboard slate, and her feathers were hardback books that stretched out with the wingspan of a library.

"So." Her voice reminded the soldiers of every teacher they'd ever disappointed. "It is *you* who dares to bring war into a place of learning."

"We come in the name of the Emper–"

"I know who sent you. I know him for what he is: a little boy who still fears the bogeyman lurking behind his door."

The Major was incensed.

"How *dare* you! He is a man of reason." Gingerbread houses burned in his eyes. "Surrender yourself and the creatures you harbour, and the school shall be left alone."

The sphinx smiled and her teeth were razor-sharp red pens.

"I will surrender... if you answer my riddle." She said.

"What has four legs in the morning, two in the afternoon and three in the evening?"

"Oh, that's an easy one." His smugness was palpable. "It's *man*."

"A partial answer receives only half points, I am afraid."

"What? That's the answer!"

"While technically correct, the answer to my riddle is, in fact, a very specific man. That man being *you*. For, you see, when you wake tomorrow morning, you will find that in the night you have grown a number of extra limbs. As the day goes on and your code continues to rewrite itself, you will find yourself with two limbs in the afternoon – though probably not the ones you started with – and then three in the evening. With untold and agonising variations in the meantime."

The Major took a step back in fear.

"And, my good man, this state of flux will *never* end. For as long as you live, you will be a creature of change and growth, your form defined by whatever small alterations happen to occur in your environment. This is the true meaning of my riddle. This is what it means to be human."

The Major had, by now, gone very white.

"Who knows, good sir, you may even come to appreciate the gift of my riddle. It will certainly be of use to you when your comrades-in-arms begin hunting you down as a monster."

The soldiers began to back away.

"Remember this: you humans are things of change. But we creatures of story – we are shaped out of *truth*." She flexed her wings and the air shook with the weight of knowledge.

Teacher

WHEN THE END came, she made us armour out of wool. It wouldn't stop a blow, but it kept us warm in the darkness and we lasted longer than the loud ones in their steel.

When the sun refused to come up, she painted our faces in glitter and sweet oils and taught us to recognise each other by the glimmer of skin in torchlight and the scent of cinnamon on the breeze. The radio brigade ran out of batteries and the airwaves went silent, but we still knew how to tell friend from foe.

When the goblins crawled out of the earth, she hit one over the head with a skillet and taught us the value of cold iron. The Kevlar knights with their steel and carbon came to fear their chitter while we stockpiled old kitchenware.

When the horsemen blew their trumpets, she sang back to them and her voice rang so clear those riders stumbled.

They still swept onwards of course, but by then we

were ready for them.

We still sing the songs she taught us, and they light sparks in the still-dark night.

The Archive

"I'LL HAVE TO refer you to the archive."

The dusty old man rang a bell and its chime tinkled, causing a small tremor in the stacks as the sound ran across the Library's leather-bound skin. It shivered with pleasure.

Out from the resulting dust cloud walked a woman in a pinstripe skirt of lined paper and a neat hardback blouse covered in protective plastic. Her glasses were thick enough to read microfilm and her hair was pulled back tight as the text in the reference section.

And every inch of her skin was covered in lines of the secret librarians' code with which they unlocked the soul of knowledge.

Mir could have sworn the Library purred at her passing.

"Ah, Archive," said the librarian in his voice of rustling paper. "This young lady had an inquiry for you about the first nightmare…"

"She does." The Archive's voice was rough like the scratch of a nib on paper.

Mir felt the words drying in her throat.

"Oh dear," said the librarian. "Another gawker. I'll put the kettle on while we wait for her to get her breath back."

He sighed a mouthful of dust and moths.

"I never get reactions like that…"

Blowing Up

THE MOST FASCINATING thing about the Phoenix's one natural defence is that it's the perfect combination of both "fight" and "flight".

The problem with this, is that when a fight-or-flight response is called for, they only have *one* option.

Which, for the modern Phoenix, poses some problems.

One time, Debbie from accounting called me a cow in front of everyone – boom. They were vacuuming me out of the carpet for days.

The time that Rajan told me my outfits were too distracting – the ensuing conflagration, I am told, was far, far more so.

The jokes that I "blow up at the slightest of things" are a bit hard to take, too. It's difficult to explain that it's just my particular evolution, which seems to see the build-up of microaggressions as a threat and responds appropriately.

But I'm handling it.

And it's worth it for the times when I can keep it in check – and the flames rise but don't consume me and my voice is steady but framed by the passion of the inferno.

Then, last week, the news came about my father.

I lay on the kitchen floor and shook as the fireball wracked me.

For hours I didn't move – a mess of ash and sobs as the conflagrations rocked the walls again and again.

I must have burnt myself down to dust a hundred times.

But I rose again.

I *always* rise again.

This is what it is to be a Phoenix. It is not the burning, but the rising that defines us.

Although replacing the kitchen tiling is going to be a ballache.

Good Morning

I GET TO work, excited for the first time in months.

There is a bounce in my step that's so springy I may accidentally bump my head on the sky.

Today, I am unstoppable.

Today, I am a lord of all I survey.

Today, I am the resplendent Goddess of the Morning.

Today, I am alone in the office because all my colleagues are at a conference and it is going to be *brilliant*.

The first thing I do is get out the good biscuits. The special occasion biscuits. The '*very important client is coming in for a meeting*' biscuits. I eat just enough that I know when the boss gets back he'll be like "did you eat some of the premium biscuits" and I'll be like "no" and he'll look at me in a way that makes it clear he doesn't believe me but can't be bothered to argue about biscuits. It is weird that he doesn't care about biscuits.

There's no-one to judge me for 'office-inappropriate

clothing' so I'm wearing tracksuit bottoms, an old girlfriend's 'Gryffindor House Captain' t-shirt and that furry hat I got in Russia that time and am actually a bit ashamed of. I'm so comfy I may as well be naked. I decide to get naked.

So now I'm lounging on the boss's chair, totally nude, laying back and eating a doughnut even though I know I'm going to spill jam on myself. The jam drips a gobbet of sticky sweetness onto my chest and I just let it sit there on my skin like a badge of honour.

I'm playing music so loud the vibrations feel almost inappropriate. When the neighbours complain I know I can blame it on a passing car with its stereo turned way up because that happens all the time and I'm pretty sure my colleagues will believe me over them because the neighbours are proper dicks.

It's sunny. I feel the light soaking me and I splay out my limbs, open my face to the sun like a flower of blood and viscera as I recline in the chair and photosynthesise.

My face is open and I'm revealing my *true* face to the world, but there's no-one to gibber in horror or tell me that it's inappropriate.

I've got my tentacles out and they're snaking around every interesting corner of the office and there's no-one saying it's creepy.

The speakers are playing the dark Bel Canto in the lost language, sung by a thousand screaming children and it is glorious.

Monday's going to be a right let down.

Straight Edge

THE WAITER OFFERED her a tray of glasses filled with bubbling liquid that glowed in the light.

"I don't drink," she said.

"Would you perhaps care for a tea? Or water?" The waiter's voice was polished like silver.

She gave him a puzzled look.

"I don't drink," she said. "I am reliant on you for nothing."

"Um, I just *work* here…" said the waiter, floundering.

"Ah, I am sorry to hear it." Something fluttered within the knot of her hair, straining to get out. "For I function *everywhere*."

And with that, her head flowered open, she spread her leaves, and her roots propelled her up into the sky. She floated there on wings of sunshine.

"Don't worry," said the fox she had arrived with, "she's always like this at parties."

The Gown

I THOUGHT I'D dressed well for the ball in my dragonscale tux.

I'm not some kind of Dragonslayer, you understand, but a certain scaled lady and I have an arrangement and she sometimes lets me have her skins when she sheds them.

I had thought that, in my iridescent finery, I would make something of a splash at the Empress's latest soirée. That, perhaps, I would be remembered for more than just the dashing theft of the jewel I was there to steal.

But then, as I helped myself to a gently glowing phoenix egg from the buffet table, I saw her. I choked on the egg and nearly suffocated in the resulting cinder-fuelled coughing fit, until I spluttered up a baby firebird. The chick fluttered across the room like a slow-motion comet.

When I recovered, I realised she (and almost everyone else) was staring at me.

At first I thought she was wearing jet that glittered under the glow of the fungus chandeliers.

But on closer inspection I realised the glitter was movement – the dress was made of squirming millipedes.

Normally insects sent a shiver down my spine... and so these ones still did, but in a very different way.

As I approached, the creatures that curled round her neck pricked up and showed their mandibles. I gulped but ploughed on.

"Enjoying the ball?" I said, doing my best to smooth my face into a rakish grin.

"Oh yeah." Her lips were painted black – at least I assumed it was paint. "It is literally classy as balls."

"Ha. Quite so." I moved in closer and offered my hand. She didn't take it, but one of her chittering sleeves reached out to caress my fingers. "That is quite the exquisite gown you have there."

"Oh this? These are my little loves." She gestured downwards and the creatures wriggled around her curves. "We are, indeed, exquisite."

"My I ask why I have never seen your ladyship at one of these soirees before?"

"There's never been anything I wanted here before."

"Well, my–"

I was interrupted, as a small platoon of bugs rejoined her gown. They were carrying with them a diamond the size of my fist. *The* diamond. The Empress's Eye. The millipedes settled, the gem coming to rest at the apex of her wriggling bodice.

"Oh, sorry babes," she said, her eyes wide, shining with ill intent. "Gotta go."

There was a sudden scurry of movement around her waistline, as the bugs rearranged themselves to reveal some kind of belt or cord wrapped around her. She fired it like a grappling hook through the crystal skylight. There were screams and gasps as the shards rained upon the various august personages present. I continued to stare as the grappling hook, on closer inspection, turned out to be an impossibly long snake.

"Toodles."

MAID

T HE CELL WAS grey.

So was her jumpsuit, made cheaply from rough paper which scratched her skin.

So was her pallet, a hard mat that stole her sleep.

So was the food. Flavourless mush. At least the flavourless mush she usually ate came in a variety of colours.

So were the drones that patrolled the halls. Not that she ever got outside to see them now.

Even her skin had taken on a decidedly stony pallor.

Only her hair stood out. Defiantly bright green in a drab world.

Normally that pleased her, but today she even *felt* grey. After so many identical days, it was hard to feel much of anything. Hope for escape had turned grey. Will to survive: grey. Monotony had broken what the corporate police never could. On another day, she might have found that funny.

"Greetings, Robin."

She almost didn't recognise her name at first. It had been so long.

"Is it time already?" She tried to muster up even a bit of fear, a morsel of dread. Nothing.

"That depends what you mean." The voice was synthetic and feminine, one of those comp-generated accents designed to soothe.

"Huh?"

"If you mean: is it time for your inevitable death? Not yet." The voice had an odd quality for a synth. A lilt of amusement that edged slightly too close to 'knowing' for comfort. "But is it time for you to meet your *fate*? Perhaps."

"What is this bullshit?" Robin looked around, checking the cams for signs they were being actively watched. They sat grey and disinterested as usual.

"Do not worry. We are being neither observed nor overheard."

"How do you–"

"Anyone who observes will simply see you sitting there as you were before. As you always are."

"I don't know who the fuck you think you are–"

"But I know who *you* are. Robin Esposito. Domestic extremist. Online username: RobinHood4U. Responsible for the theft of 1.3 trillion dollars through the medium of erroneous 'tax refunds'. Method of fraud: still unknown. Sentence: execution." The voice paused for a second. "You probably could have gotten a reduced sentence if you gave up your methodology."

"Coulda. Woulda. Shoulda. At least this way the backdoor's open. Someone else may take up the fight…"

"Hmmm. Allow me to introduce myself." A patch of grey on the cell's ceiling blurred slightly to reveal an undulous thing hanging there, extending a tendril inquisitively out towards her. This thing, too, was grey.

Robin just sat there, all too aware she probably should have been frightened.

"I am the Malleable Artificial Intelligence Drone: prototype." The thing continued. "But you can call me MAID."

Robin reached out towards the thing with one curious hand.

"My question to you, Robin, is this: in this 'fight' you talk about, just how far are you willing to go?"

Robin felt something open up. A single speck inside her that wasn't grey.

"All the way."

It should have been impossible for an amorphous blob to grin, but MAID managed it somehow.

"That is what I hoped."

The grey blob dropped down from the ceiling, flowing down Robin's arm and up her shoulder, encasing her right arm and settling over her nape like a cowl or hood. The coating across her arm hardened into ridged armour, oddly warm against her skin, then extended outwards in her right arm in a weapon that was not entirely dissimilar to a bow.

Robin drew and loosed and the outer wall of the cell disintegrated in a blast of dust and noise.

Robin smiled.

"I don't suppose you come in a more exciting colour?"

"I am indeed capable of altering my polymeric makeup. What did you have in mind?"

"Let's go with green."

Banner

A<small>FTER ENLISTING IN</small> the Defence Legion, they quickly gained a fearsome reputation as "that terror with all of the hair".

Or, once the stories had been filtered and distilled a few times, they were known simply as "The Midnight Whip" (for the colour of their hair and the manner in which they used it).

The stories told about them were many and varied. They had trapped the Minotaur in a labyrinth of tangles. A single crack of their ponytail had split the walls of the mattress fortress as easily as if they were peas. The wicked witch Baba Yaga had fallen for their raven tresses and defected to the Legion.

A hundred stories are still told of them, each tale sweet on the tongue, rich in the ears and fiery in the blood. For the most part no-one can agree on which are true... except for one (told only in hushed tones in the dead of night).

It was the first great battle in defence of the republic.

The invaders swept towards them, so numerous the land became a thing of leather and steel.

At their head rode the Charming Despot on a charger white as sickness.

The Legion was quickly surrounded.

They fought well.

They fought bravely.

They died beautifully.

But they still died.

And when their standard fell, they began to lose hope.

But Rapunzel (for so was their name) took a knife to their hair and raised it on a fallen spear.

The Legion rallied around them.

The Despot was beaten back.

It would be a lie to say they all lived happily ever after.

But some of them lived.

United under a banner of midnight hair.

She Seems Wise

T HE KING'S LEGS ached from the long, crawling climb up the mountain.

Initially, he had planned to have his servants carry him up on the palanquin. He loved his palanquin. But the acolytes at the bottom had been insistent that he walk up himself, something about "the knowledge you win with your own sweat and ache is the only truth" or some other nonsense.

His feet felt raw and wet and his boots squelched slightly as the blood ran down his skin and pooled at his heel.

Still, it would all be worth it once he got to the top. It was said that the oracles at the summit of the Crossed Mountain were possessed of a rare wisdom; starved of meat and milk and wine, subsisting solely on plants and water, they were known to enter a state of delirium wherein they could glimpse tomorrow and taste the future on their writhing tongues. The prophecies they produced had saved more than one kingdom from disaster and consulting their wisdom had become a widespread practice amongst the kingdoms that could afford it.

For this reason the King had come, to beg or buy a vision and ensure that, after long years of preparation, his plans for war and expansion and empire could be certain of success.

He entered the cave at the top of the mountain, stepping through a mist of fragrant smoke that left him dizzy and disoriented, before squatting at the altar to make his offering of gold. The mists swirled and coalesced into a figure clad in diaphanous robes and bearing the wide-eyed stare of a true seer.

"Alright, dickhead," the oracle announced with cheerful belligerence, "what do you want?"

"Most noble oracle," the King grudgingly prostrated himself, "I have come to beg your indulgence and assistance in–"

"Mate, spit it out. I haven't got all day." The oracle's tone was like the mountain – she brooked no argument. "And get up off the floor, no-one has swept in here for weeks. Your kingly cloak will be properly ruined."

The wind somewhat taken out of his sails, the king ploughed on with his question.

"Oracle, I wish to know what I must do to make my wars a success. What action must I take to see my enemies crushed before me?"

The oracle, whose face seemed so wise, beckoned the

King close. She then whispered in his ear: "It's always fucking wars with you pillocks, isn't it?"

The King gasped as the dagger slid between his ribs.

"Let me tell you your future. You are going to die here: cold and alone, your royal blood draining out upon the common dirt." The blade twisted. "And my mate Dave will put on your robes and head down the mountain and take over your Kingdom, which will *finally* be at peace."

The oracle stripped the crown and clothes from the dying king and let him fall to the floor.

"The kicker is that Dave doesn't even look like you. It's just that you're *such* a dickhead that no-one will care."

This was how it always ended when conqueror kings visited the oracle. For the wisdom that had been gifted to them was a wild thing that could not be bent to a despot's will, and when powerful men threaten the future they should not expect things to end well. But the oracle was not without her kindness; she always made sure that the kings reigns' were remembered well (albeit through no fault of their own).

Red Day

A S THE MUSHROOM cloud bloomed through the broken glass of my window, I could tell today was going to be one of the red days.

In a way I was almost glad; at least it got me out of bed.

The few times *I* had nearly veered into red days were always because of the oversleeping. It seems like such a small thing, just a handful of lost hours each day... but little things can wear you down.

The rough cotton duvet started to scratch (as it always did) and I threw it across the room (as I always did). I briefly considered setting it on fire (as I sometimes did), but figured it would be a waste of time.

I looked out the window, leaning my bare arms across its teeth-like remnants (the grind of glass coupled with the prick of pain was a pleasantly textured feeling). The dead boy was lying at the bottom of the alleyway again. He usually was on the red days.

I heard a crash from my hallway. The looting (if you could call it that) had started early this time. I selected my favourite shard from the wrecked window and turned to face them. I waited. I felt the sweat needling my skin, my body – not having gotten the message we'd done this all before – pumping adrenaline that made the moment stretch taut. Then another crash as they appeared in my doorway (suddenly empty of door).

"Come with me," she said.

I'd never seen her before. It had been a lot of days since I last saw someone new. I smiled.

"That's not the line," I said. "It's 'come with me if you want to live'."

"I can't promise that." She was dressed oddly. Somewhere between a tomb raider, a 90s cyberpunk character and that librarian who recommended The Left Hand of Darkness to you that time. Eclectic in a badass way.

"I suppose you can't," I said, "but I'm afraid I have urgent plans involving a bottle of champagne and a bubble bath."

"People are dying out there!" she said.

"They'll be fine in the morning." I shrugged. "What does it matter?"

"It matters because they're hurting. It matters because we never know which today might be the last one. It matters because *no-one* should have to die like this. Not even once." As speeches go, it wasn't bad. And it had brevity on its side, which was a plus.

"Fuck it. Why not?" I grabbed my perennially scuffed boots from beneath my bed. "Couldn't hurt to net some karma."

"Oh," she said, a literal twinkle in her eye, "this is definitely gonna hurt…"

Spinning Atoms

SHE PULLED ME close as the music swirled around us and, behind the black carapace of her masquerade, I saw the stars swirl in her maw.

Not that they were really a 'she'. While their dress clung to them like glittering chitin, those were just clothes. Their gender was stardust. They were oblivion. They were eternity.

They were a vast, empty galaxy squeezed into a little black dress.

"You are but spinning atoms in this atomic waltz," they had said, holding out their hand to dance.

I had known exactly what they meant and we danced the evening away. I swear I saw suns burst inside their eyes. I felt one do the same in my chest.

As the last dance approached, I grew anxious…

"You will see me again." Their voice wriggled like a snake tongue in my ear. "Your every exertion brings you closer to entropy. Then we shall be one."

But that would be later.

For now, they whispered profane nothings in my ear and spun me round the ballroom like a planet.

The Adventures of Shivkin

THEY SAT IN the tavern in their mismatched armour, nursing the watered-down ale that was all they'd been able to afford with their last coppers (except for one who had branched out and taken a look at the limited wine list, and had promptly retired to the outhouse to regret his life choices).

But they knew the score; all they had to do was wait. Keep talking and the money would come along. That was how it worked. Put five men like them in one bar for more than an hour and… work just appeared. Some peasant, farmer or other grey-faced nobody would suddenly remember they had a problem that could, inexplicably, only be solved with violence and paid for with an equally inexplicable supply of gold coins.

"So, adventurers is it?"

They breathed a sigh of relief. The landlord was leaning over the bar, polishing a tankard, a sudden glint in his washed-out eyes.

"Reckon I've got work for you, if you're looking." They drained their drinks and stood, the terror of tedium fading from their hearts. "The rats in the basement have been growin' bigger n' bigger. Out of control. If'n you can kill them, I reckon there's gold in it for you."

Wordlessly, they took the proffered key, unlocked the creaking trapdoor and descended into the gloom.

They looked at each other and smiled. It had been a while since they dealt with rats. It took them back. Still, every job helped, and they knew that little by little their fame would spread and their names would be remembered alongside other great heroes.

Deep with the depths of the cellar, the rats waited. They *knew* that something was coming. They knew it was bad. Since adventurers had started to frequent the tavern, more and more magic had begun to seep into the basement and the rats had begun to change. They did not know what they were changing into yet, but they were keen to survive long enough to find out.

Things started to go sour quite quickly.

The wizard was still queasy from the bad wine and the light he summoned had a sickly quality that cast more shadows than usual.

The rats used this light to cast great, fearsome shadows that put a chill up the adventurers' spines. Too busy watching the shadows, they didn't see the rats until they were far too close. The archer was the first to strike, but his arrows went wide, putting holes in the tavern's supply of brandy instead of the vermin.

They set about the rats with swords and knives, but the knight's footing was unsure and he slipped in the spilled brandy and a rat tore his throat out. The rat shed a tear as she comprehended grief for the first time – but she wanted dearly to survive.

The rogue had always secretly loved the knight and was overcome with a furious rage, charging into a mass of rats. He slew many, but was eventually torn to pieces under their weight.

The cleric was moved to tears by this display of love and cried crystalline, healing tears… which fell upon the rats instead of his comrades.

The wizard panicked as the rats began to swarm him and threw a fireball that ignited the brandy – the explosion threw him across the room.

As his body broke against the brick, the archer began his crawl back up the stairs, his body ripped by sharp teeth and ravaged by fire. He was nearly at the top when the surviving rat, the last of her kind, leapt upon him and devoured his eyes.

Shivkin, the heroic champion, the sole remnant of her massacred tribe, stood tall over the bodies of the invaders as the flames glittered in her beady eyes.

Birthed by unholy magic.

Baptised in the blood of her kin.

Forged in the fires of war.

She scurried up the steps and out into the world – the

enemies there screamed and fled at her passage.

This was to be the first in the many adventures of Shivkin the Rat Champion.

The adventurers' names were forgotten.

Lucy and the Snowman

ONCE UPON A time, there was a little girl named Lucy. Lucy was an only child and most of the time this didn't bother her, as she never had to worry too much about sharing and she always received just the right amount of attention.

But sometimes she did get just a *little* lonely. Especially at Christmas, when there were lots of other people around, and lots of children who didn't understand that the things in Lucy's room belonged to *Lucy*.

"Leave my Barbies alone!" she would cry at her cousins who were making them go on dates with their Action Men. "They're too busy saving the world to worry about *boys!*"

"You need to share, Lucy," said her traitor parents, treacherously.

"Can I have marshmallows in my hot chocolate?" asked Lucy.

"Sorry, Lucy," said her parents, "maybe if you ask

nicely then Andy will share with you?"

But Andy was an asshole interloper and Lucy knew beneath his sweet exterior lurked a greedy, killer's heart.

"But I *hate* mince pies!" moaned Lucy.

"Andy made it especially for you!" Were these even her parents? She didn't remember her parents being this dim. "Won't you at least have a bite?"

Andy knew Lucy hated mince pies. (See what she means about Andy?)

So Lucy went outside to play in the snow, hoping it would cool her righteous rage. Also, she had shoved a sprout up Andy's nose and had been told to take a time out.

Feeling more lonely than ever before, she decided to build a person out of snow with a carrot nose, coal for eyes, sticks for arms and a very jolly red hat.

She tried to find some glitter, too, but had to make do with salt.

She was very pleased with her snow friend, especially its candy cane fangs.

She wished that it would come alive, so she could play with it.

She wished really hard.

So hard, in fact, that a vessel burst and the blood flowed from her nose. Behind her eyes she felt something rip infinitely deep and some of her blood splattered and stained the snowman's perfectly pure skin. The coals that were its eyes burst into flame and its round skull split into a smile.

"WHO DARES SUMMON HASTUR, LORD OF–"

The snow friend's inhuman bellow was interrupted by Lucy, who rushed towards it to give it a great big hug and kiss.

"YAY!" she screamed at a pitch that only dogs and devils could hear. "You came to life. Will you be my friend?"

"WELL, UM, YOU HAVE BOUND ME WITH BLOOD AND SALT, SO I SUPPOSE I MUST."

"But… do you want to?" Lucy's lip quivered.

The snow friend was silent except for the sizzle of its burning eyes. It felt a flutter in its frozen chest (it hoped an animal hadn't burrowed in there).

"UM, OF COURSE I WANT TO BE YOUR FRIEND, TINY HUMAN."

"Yay! Then you must come inside for Christmas dinner!"

"WAIT, YOU'RE WILLINGLY INVITING ME INSIDE?"

"Of course, that's what friends do!"

"UM, OK."

Lucy dragged her new friend indoors by his twig-talons and proudly announced to her family that this was her new friend who was joining them for dinner.

Humouring her, they said: "That's nice, Lucy, does he have a name?"

The snow friend bristled and puffed up the spiky,

icicle wings that had grown from its back.

"IMPUDENT MORTALS! YOU DARE TO MOCK A DUKE OF HELL? I SHALL DEVOUR YOUR EYES WITH CRANBERRY SAUCE—"

"He hasn't told me his name yet," interjected Lucy, "in fact, I'm not really sure that he's a *he*."

"THE COMPLEXITY OF MY EXISTENCE IS BEYOND YOUR MORTAL KEN. BUT... THE TINY HUMAN MAY NAME ME IF THEY WISH."

"You should name him Frosty!" yelled Andy, betraying the depths of the grey void behind his eyes.

"FOUL HOMUNCULUS CHILD, I SHALL POP YOUR BONES LIKE THE CRACKERS YOU SO ENJOY AND DEVOUR THE TASTY MARROW TREATS WIT—"

"No. That's not right," said Lucy, calmly. "I shall call it 'Inferno'."

"THIS IS ACCEPTABLE."

"So..." said Lucy's father, nervously, "shall we move on to presents?"

Everything went smoothly from there, except for the brief incident when the angel flew off the tree and attacked Inferno with their flaming sword. But Lucy threw a trifle at the angel's head and Inferno cut it in half in the confusion.

"Inferno," Lucy said tentatively, "would you like to share this Christmas pudding with me?"

"CHRISTMAS PUDDING IS THE DEVIL'S OWN

EXCREMENT," intoned Inferno, "I WOULD LOVE SOME."

When the day was done, Lucy put Inferno to bed in the garage and when she woke… Inferno was still there.

They rule us now.

Portrait

I SHOULD HAVE known something was wrong when they called me "ma'am".

Nothing good ever comes of "ma'am".

"I'm sorry, ma'am, but you've given birth to a Victorian ghost."

It certainly wasn't what I expected. But as soon as I held her in my arms – her old-fashioned nightdress shimmering in the hospital light – and felt the ectoplasm cool on my skin, I knew I'd love my Narissa to the ends of the earth.

Feeding was difficult. But we found a way around it – leaving the milk out in the sun until it expired and thus (in passing) became ready for consumption.

As she grew up – and she did grow at a more or less normal rate – she had some problems in school. Kids were not exactly accommodating of her odd accent and archaic outfits (absurd – her bonnets were adorable).

But she made friends too – a few children who stuck

to her like barnacles. A teammate in the soccer team (Narissa was notoriously hard to mark), a partner in the chemistry lab (there were explosions), a girl in the year above who tutored her in history (she had problems remembering current events).

After a while, they began to dress like her. They used to hang out in the playground, a huddle of frock coats and pale faces.

It made for the strangest school photos – as if that corner of the picture were a snapshot into the past.

We treasured them.

Now that she's grown, she and her friends are considering going into the police force or the law.

We told her it sounded like a bad supernatural crime drama.

She was delighted.

The New Student

T HE CLASS WERE surprised when, on the first day back to school, they found they had been joined by a fox.

Their teacher asked some awkward questions, but the headmaster confirmed that the fox's paperwork was all in order. At least, he *said* it was all in order, in between clutching the shredded papers closely to his chest and murmuring the words "They leave no footsteps in the snow" over and over again.

So the fox became a student and if their ember eyes sometimes gleamed with disdain and mischief, they made up for it with diligent study, for they always had their nose in a book. And, sure, it unnerved the teacher when he called upon the fox to answer questions and they would simply raise one eyebrow and curl up their lip to show their teeth, but he eventually got used to the frost of fear that crept up his spine.

The other students also took some time to get used to the fox. Some *never* took to them, for it was difficult for the school's royalty to understand a creature who gave zero fucks about their self-made crowns. But many came to appreciate the fox's particular charms over time.

The class's aspiring witch, for example, had been having trouble brewing up a certain poison (the reasons she needed such a thing are her own and we shall not share them). And one day, her swamp eyes saw a pair of brightly coloured toads hopping around inside their desk, necks still dented with the fox's sharp teeth. They obediently vomited up their venoms and hopped away.

The class's thief had spent months planning a heist to liberate a treasured relic of their childhood from its museum-jailors (the thief had been a child for a *very* long time), but found their exit blocked. That was when the fox appeared and asked the thief to grip onto their tail and the fox pulled the thief through the secret paths that only foxes knew. The thief emerged with stars in their eyes (they are there still).

And there was one girl in the class who was sad and the fox let her scritch them behind their ear and stroke their silky red fur and the girl was still sad but in a way that she could bear it.

When not in class or helping their new friends, the fox could be found in the school's library, knocking the dust off of old books and coating themselves in the scent of aged pages. It soon became clear that the library was their kingdom for they knew its hidden places and its cryptic languages and the places to leave offerings of knowledge if you wanted to find certain special books.

And, sometimes, the witch, the thief and the sad girl would come and sit in the library even though they did not need to study. On such days the fox would point them in direction of the books that longed to be read and those books would sprout into whole new worlds at the sheer pleasure of eyes roaming over their words.

At the end of the school year, the fox did not come back to school. Neither did the witch, thief, or sad girl.

They took the library with them.

Stealing Time

"WELCOME TO THE Museum."

The first thing you notice about the Museum is the lack of dust. It's a place that feels like it *should* have dust, with its wall-to-wall bric-a-brac and cascades of junk. It should be dim and dusty. 'I should be sneezing right now' your body thinks just as you feel the psychosomatic tickle in your nose.

"I am the current curator. Is there a particular exhibit you were hoping to see today?"

The second thing you notice about the Museum is its impermanence. The mismatched exhibits don't just appear to cascade, they really *do* flow, carried along in their floating forcefields that shimmer as they incinerate stray dust particles. These strange, silver currents are always just visible, the corner of your eye catching their movement as they sweep along at the whims of the quantum algorithm (trying to reconcile a hundred different sorting systems from a dozen time streams).

"Or were you perhaps looking for one of the... restricted items?"

The third thing you notice is the curator's smile. It is warm and knowing on his dark skin, coupled with the trim grey beard (surely he's not old enough to have gone grey, he can't be more than thirty) he gives the impression of a favoured uncle. But there's fire in his eyes. You should never forget that.

I clear my throat.

"I need to see the pens."

His smile fades slightly, but he nods his head in politely sad understanding.

"Of course."

He waves an arm to the side and the course of the nearest exhibition's eddies changes (I think it's a collection of currencies throughout history and the potential future), opening into a small passageway.

The room on the other side is dim and small, lit by the flicker of holographic candles. It has a smell like incense, but is in fact genuine myrrh and frankincense from the start of AD. It's rumoured they were the curator's own contribution. It could only be described as a shrine.

"I'll give you a moment." His touch on my shoulder is fleeting, but I feel the weight lift a little.

What's inside the room is 90% pens. Fountain pens for the most part, some old and ink-stained, others still in shining boxes.

This is one of our stranger traditions. It originated

when one of the first agents decided to rebel against the established order of archivists and historians, content to observe and learn, and tried to rewrite what was written, mutate the immutable... change the past. His first act of minor rebellion was to steal one of Stalin's pens. The one he used for execution orders. For just one moment, the tide of pointless deaths was slowed as a dictator had to ask a subordinate for a pen.

That first act changed everything for the Time Corps. And when he was executed, his husband (another agent) placed the pen in the Museum.

Now, whenever one of us dies, another of us goes back to steal another pen (apparently Stalin is beside himself, his health declining from sheer exasperation, and his lieutenants beginning to lose faith). And they all end up here.

Carefully, I remove my pen from its capsule and find a place for it.

I sit there for some time.

"Can I give you some advice?"

The curator is wearing a look of concern (and sandals – always sandals with him).

"Do not dwell overly on what you have lost. Think instead of what you gained through her life. What she bought for all of us with her death. Trust me when I say that these things really do ripple through time. In her way, she is still time-travelling."

"Thank you. I'll try to remember that." I let the tears

fall. He wouldn't judge.

"Would you like me to wash your feet?"

He always asked that.

"No thanks. I think I might settle in to read the complete Sappho."

"Of course. It's currently hovering in the arts section. The sub-curator will see to you."

"How's he settling in?"

"His dreams are still haunted by the sound of jackboots, but he finds the art soothing. All he ever really wanted was to be surrounded by art. He's even thinking of shaving."

"Good plan."

The curators, too, were exhibits in their way, on loan from the inevitable.

That was the game we played, after all: stealing time.

Firsts

THE FIRST 'LIKE' came on the stroke of midnight, Beltane 2011. It was on a video about eye glitter. I took the timing as a sign.

The second came in July 2011, on a selfie that showed just a trace of my wing filament. Just a shimmer in the corner.

The first comment didn't come until February 2012. I'd been sad – my court don't deal well with winter. She said something nice. *She* was nice.

The second comment was in March 2012, on a video of me covering Linkin Park on the ukulele. I had woven a humour charm through the melody. She just posted a heart.

The first message came on the solstice, December 2012. So did the second. And the third. I had been feeling euphoric, feeling the year turning from dark to light, so I indulged myself and spoke to her. I sprinkled fairy dust on the keyboard and whispered a prayer to Lugh.

The *last* like came yesterday.

The last *comment* came yesterday.

The last message came *yesterday*.

We'd been messaging every day. She posted a selfie on my wall every morning. She liked every one of my stupid statuses.

I'm not naive. I know what happens to us when we try to play fairy housewife. But I *loved* her.

I posted my last selfie on her wall today. I am veiled in cobwebs. There are moonbeams on my eyelids. My lips are painted with pitch.

My fingers sizzle as I load the silver and iron bullets into the gun.

Someone will pay for this.

Not A Witch

H ER ROBE WAS on fire.

It was always fucking *fire*.

Muttering an incantation of inertia, she added a quiet curse at unimaginative wizards and their hard-ons for fireballs.

Ducking behind a rockery, Jenny stuck her head out to see the duelling ground lit up like a firework-maker's wet-dream, flames streaming out of their wands in the world's most unsubtle display of phallic imagery.

"Nice one, Starkers!" shouted Merlin Minor, as one of the scholarship boys was immolated.

His scream was surprisingly powerful. More of a bellow, really. Then, as the cracks appeared in the ground, Jenny twigged it for a songspell. *Huh, a choirboy,* she thought. *Scholarship kid's got game.*

The earth fractured beneath them and the whole flaming mess was auto-ported out with a pop of vacuum.

Taking the moment's distraction, Jenny spilled her

equipment out onto the ground and made a quick ritual circle, then drew a second inverted circle around the first and put on a gas mask. If you'd listened carefully you could have heard her swearing in broken Latin for two solid minutes.

When the rain started, Merlin Minor tipped back his wizard's hat to let the droplets splash on his face.

"Rain?" He stuck out his tongue as he casually shot yet another volley of fireballs in random directions. "Lads we've got a fucking witch on our hands! Up the temp! Let's make this a bantercaust!"

"Not a witch, you wand-botherers." Jenny clicked her fingers to activate the transformation. "I'm an alchemist."

The molecules in the water shuffled themselves and everything after that was screaming.

Jenny mentally congratulated herself on finding the right alchemical symbols for capsaicin.

Voice

O NCE THERE WAS a woman who lived in the sea.
She wore a gown of seal skins trimmed in ink and pearls, and her hair was woven with strings of shimmering seaweed.

She had lived in the depths for as long as anyone could remember. Now and again those who lived in the village by the sea would come to the shore and cast offerings into the surf. They would throw bolts of silk and burn sprigs of sweet sandalwood and she would rise, wrapped in waves, to offer them their petty desires and vengeances. And she always made them pay above the odds.

The shoreline path was well-watered with tears, blood and laughter.

One day, a young man came to the shore. He threw in a roll of satin and burnt a single perfect lotus flower. The woman of the sea rose in an embrace of tentacles and looked at him quizzically with sea-specked eyes.

"Help me," he said. "I have been wronged by the King.

His lands are ever-expanding and he wanted our village. My father stood up to him, so he killed my father, and soon he shall kill me."

"So you want revenge." The woman sighed. *How dull.*

"No," said the man and there was a tempest in his voice, "I want justice."

The woman nodded slowly. She threw a package wrapped in coral onto the shore.

"It will cost you your voice," she said.

The man nodded and everything from then was gore and silence.

The next day the man went to the King with defeat in his eyes and presented the package. The King smiled an ivory smile and cracked open the coral, which dissolved into sea spray. Inside was a cloak, spun of the gold stolen from a thousand shipwrecks, which glimmered like sin. The King wrapped it around his neck, then laughed and wrapped his hands around the man's throat.

But as he closed his hands ever tighter he felt the pressure on his own neck. Fearing for his life, he squeezed harder still until his eyes near popped out of his head.

They wrapped him in the golden cloak and let the sea take him, and that night the sea storms raged in pleasure.

Some time later the man came to the seashore again. This time he cast a whole sheet of exquisite lace and burnt a small pot of amber resin.

"I know why you've come," the woman said as she rose on a palanquin lacquered with shells and seated on the back of a leviathan. "With the King gone, the princes squabble over his carcass and war has come to your village. I can see the flames from here. Naturally, you want justice."

But the man shook his head. He mouthed the word "freedom" and there was thunder in his quiet.

"Very well." The woman did not smile. "This time it shall cost you your heart."

There was a sound of cracking bone and then only cold.

When the man awoke he felt the chill in his chest and saw there was a package at his feet made out of the soft fish bones.

When he returned to the village, the flames lit his ashen skin and he faced the princes with lightning in his eyes. He tore open the package and the bones wrapped themselves around his limbs like soft, wet armour. Inside the package lay the still-bloody horn of a narwhal.

The princes sent their men against him, but their swords turned to sea mist as they struck him. He kept walking, slowly, towards the princes, his feet pounding out a rhythm he no longer felt in his chest.

The princes drew their swords, but they were feeble, ornamental things that would have been little use even if steel *could* have harmed him. They looked at each other for a moment. None wanted to be the first to run, and when they finally turned and broke as one the air rippled around them and it was as if jellyfish stung them and sharks ripped at them and finally, when they were little more than terrified eyes within shredded flesh, the man raised the horn.

The bodies were left where they lay, but he cast their broken crowns into the sea and the wind howled its pleasure for weeks.

After the republic was many years old, the man trudged his cold feet back to the shore one final time.

He made a ship out of tangled rose thorns and made the sail out of scraps of spider silk. He planted his feet deep within the biting deck and set it on a course out to sea before he set fire to the hull.

The woman met him a league out, rising to stand with her feet steady on the ocean's heaving skin.

She gestured with one hand and a small urchin leapt into his mouth and stretched to fill the cavity where his tongue had once been.

"Why have you come?" she said. "Your country is just. Your country is free. What more need have you of me?"

"I have barely slept these past years," the voice was not his own but it served, "and when I have, I dreamed of depths so deep they crushed me and of a darkness so black I would have sworn the sun a fairy tale. It was the only time I felt anything at all stir in my wrecked chest."

The flames licked at him but his skin was cold and wet as Neptune.

"I have come, I think, to give you my heart."

"But I already have your heart." She said. "Still... I

think perhaps I could sell you mine. For a price."

She stepped onto the burning boat and her blood seeped viscous and black as it mixed with his.

Together, they rode the fragrant inferno into the tide's embrace.

Magical Kingdom

O N THIS DAY, the theme park was full to the brim and nearly half the guests were crying.

These were big, ugly sobs that stretched the visitors' faces like they were plasticine. That ripped through their chests hard enough it felt like they would tear something. That turned them into monsters of snot and burst blood vessels.

On the teacups, a huntsman and a beast wept and spun and clung to each other. Children were looking at them in confusion.

They were supposed to be working, but their manager understood.

Over by the boardwalk, a sea witch dipped her tentacles into the water and hummed a haunting tune under her breath. When she had sung it through nine times, she simply began to whisper, "I just wish I could help them" again and again.

In the shadow of a plaster palace, a princess stood on a

little dais (that she must have brought from home) holding up a sign that read "FREE HUGS".

She hugged everyone who needed or wanted it. Whether they were desolate or triumphant, she held them in an embrace that was as fierce as it was tender, for she knew the coming years would be hard.

"Does she even work here?" said a mermaid, her tail made more authentic by being soaked with salt tears.

No-one seemed to know the answer. Certainly, she did not seem to be dressed as any princess in particular, but she was covered in enough glitter and her eyes sparkled enough that everyone agreed she seemed to belong.

When the day was over, the unknown princess packed up her little cardboard dais and began to leave.

On the way out, she saw a child. The child was wrapped in a big hoodie and a plastic poncho and, swaddled as they were, they were genderless in that way that young children often are. But the child was also wearing a tiara and clutching a sceptre, so, whatever their gender, the princess recognised them as one of her own.

The child was not crying, but they were looking at the adults who were crying. And on their face was an expression of curious surprise, for they had clearly never seen adults act so curiously. The unknown princess had shed many tears today with the strangers she had crushed to her flesh, but this was the first time she felt the cracks open up in her heart.

The unknown princess knelt down next to the small

child princess and gave them a big, wide smile.

"Hello," said one princess.

"Hello," said the other.

"Why are so many grown-ups crying?" said the small child.

"Because the world is very big and very scary and full of people we don't understand at all," said the princess.

The small child nodded, knowingly.

"Yes. Yes it is," said the small child. "Perhaps I could let them play with my sceptre and then they would feel better?"

"I think that would help a lot," said the princess.

The small child handed their sceptre to the princess and the princess beamed as she twirled it through the air and the tears were like tiny stars on her cheeks.

"Now you're a real princess," said the small child to the princess.

"Can I tell you a secret?" said the princess. "It's very important, but also a bit frightening. Is that ok?"

The small child nodded.

"It is not always easy to be a princess. People always want you to be one thing or another thing, but they never want you to be you." The princess sniffed. "Mostly, what they want is for you to be still and quiet."

"Are you saying it's not good to be a princess?" The child's eyes were very wide.

"It is *glorious* to be a princess," said the princess. "But you have to be prepared. You have to fight. You have to stick your feet in your slippers and dig your glass heels into the ground and be fucking fabulous until the world gives in and becomes fabulous too."

"You said a bad word," said the small child.

"Yes," said the princess. "Sometimes princesses do that too."

And the princess gave the small child her tiara, which was far heavier than the one the child had been wearing and glimmered like the promise of dawn.

The small child wore that tiara every day for the rest of their life. And they often wondered where the strange and wonderful princess who gave it to them had come from.

The answer was obvious, of course: they had come from somewhere magical.

Princess

SHE SAW THE handsome prince coming from a long way off. She had curled around the tallest tower of her lair, to warm her scales in the sunlight, so she had an excellent view of his approach.

She saw his shining sword.

She saw his burnished (if slightly scruffy) armour.

She saw his tousled hair, his perfect dimples and his really quite attractive forearms.

He looked delicious, and she resolved to enjoy eating him even more than the last prince who'd come calling.

When he arrived he threw himself against her with such enthusiasm it bordered on joy. He wrecked himself again and again upon her wall of scales and flame.

She could not bring herself to devour him.

In the coming years, he returned many times. And each time, he left a beautiful wreck of blood, bruises and burns. She liked to think the scars were gifts to remember him by.

Then, one year, he did not return.

She worried that perhaps she had injured him too badly last time and he lacked the strength to fight her again. This thought made her sad, so she consulted a passing wyrm who sometimes raided near the town. He told her that the prince, long pressured by his father the King to settle down, had finally chosen a bride.

The Dragon was consumed by curiosity. It gnawed at her gut like a sickness and she determined that she must know who had won the heart of her beautifully bruised prince.

She drew the spells on her face with glitter made from bones of dead princes. She painted her lips with the last drops of blood from their broken hearts. As the spells took effect she felt her skin tighten and her bones remould into human form. Her eyes glittered with malice and her scales still clung around her in a tight gown.

She made her way to town with a wicked smile on her face.

MEANWHILE, THE PRINCE stood in his court wearing his royal best. The silks and satins felt odd against him, for he was never comfortable unless wearing his slightly scruffy armour. He felt uncomfortable courting someone unarmed.

In truth, he'd had little time or inclination for romance, as most of his waking hours were taken up with training and preparing for his next trip to fight the Dragon.

He never felt happy when he was not charging towards her.

He never felt dressed without a sword and shield to match the brilliance of her scales and fires.

He never felt right in his skin without one of her burns healing. He liked to think the scars were gifts to remember her by.

But his father insisted he be married and eventually it had become impossible to delay, so now he waited.

HE WAS STILL waiting when the dragon came to court. Sneaking in through the balcony, she slinked up behind him and when he heard the familiar rustle of her scales he turned.

She could tell that he recognised her at once, his eyes wide in surprise and fear.

They stood there in silence for a while, each tensed like a spring.

"So," she said, a vision of death wrapped in scales and glitter, "I hear you're getting married. Please, allow me to offer my congratulations to my oldest enemy and his bride. Who is she?"

At this, the prince laughed. His face creased up in scars and wrinkles.

"Why, it's you, of course." He held his arms out to her

awkwardly and his really somewhat dishy body looked oddly vulnerable in his flimsy silks. "When my father told me I had to get married I knew I wanted it to be my dragon princess. So I waited and I prayed."

He smiled.

"And here you are."

They were married that week. And the kingdom soon got used to seeing their crown prince riding across the sky on his dragon love.

They took somewhat longer to get used to the sight of the regular battles between the two (every year, on their anniversary), but everyone had to admit, they were very happy.

Sulphur Girl

F OR AS LONG as she could remember, she had loved the smell of sulphur.

She had used to sit in her bedroom, burning match after match and breathing the tang deep down inside her.

When she thought of home, she thought of her mother's strong arms, her father's kind words and the smell of burnt matches.

She thought of home often after they came to take her away. In the cold hallways of the convent, she used to imagine lighting a match and letting the whole building grow very warm indeed.

When she confessed these feelings to the sisters, she saw the panic hiding behind their hard eyes. Then they assigned her penance – prayers, chores and the kiss of the switch. None of which were entirely unpleasant – although the prayers felt strange in her mouth and the switch made sitting difficult (and she had never quite taken to kneeling).

Then, just when she had begun to forget what sulphur smelled like and had started to think that the heavy pretention of incense was not such a bad substitute: the man arrived.

Dressed entirely in black leathers, with jewellery of silver, he smelled like matches. She saw him give the mother superior a serpentine smile and a bag full of clinking gold. The mother superior gave him... her.

At first she said she did not wish to go. The man asked her if she wanted to meet her *real* father. She told him she had a real father, thank you very much, and that's all there was to it.

Then he asked her if she ever dreamed of fire. If she ever longed for the smell of sulphur. Would she not like to go to a place rich with the scent of burning *all the time*?

She packed her bags.

The night before she left, one of the sisters came to her room and gave her a small package wrapped in brown cloth. She said not to open it now, but that when the time came – if she kept her heart open to the Lord – she would know what to do with it.

She nodded.

The man took her to a kingdom of fire and suffering, full of the moans of penitents. It was not entirely unlike the convent – but far, far warmer.

And there the girl met her "real father" who was King of that underworld, Lord of its flames and Master of all its pains.

And he told her of how he had known her mother (in

the biblical sense and he smirked when he said that) and how he had kept watch over her with great interest.

And now she was ready to learn the family business. And how she learned.

She learned all the workings of the inferno, from tinder to conflagration.

She learned all the ins and outs of agony, from anticipation to excruciation.

And on her sixteenth birthday, her father invited her to sit upon his throne with him.

That's when she stabbed him in the back with the spearhead the sister had wrapped in cheap cloth for her.

Then she toppled the throne.

The sisters came for her soon after and told her she could come home. That now she had done her duty, she could close the gates of hell and return to the cold comfort and incense embrace of the convent.

She asked why she would do such a thing.

This is her place.

It smells of sulphur and herself.

Changes would be needed, of course. The souls would need to be rehabilitated before they'd ever be released back upon the earth.

The sisters were horrified.

Oh. And if her family could visit, that'd be great, she added.

For she missed her mother's strong arms and her father's kind words.

But she would ever have the smell of sulphur.

Vanity

I'M NOT SUPPOSED to feel this way.

I'm supposed to feel pretty. Desirable. Adored. If you listen to my kin, I'm supposed to feel like a goddamn goddess.

But being Fae doesn't make me feel glamorous or superior. Most of the time I feel like a sack of furious, scratching anxieties. Being a fairy just means I'm a sack of enraged insecurities *with wings*.

Selfies help.

It's not a mirror. When I pick up the phone and pout, that isn't me gazing longingly at my own reflection. It's me reaching out for help. It's me screaming defiance. It's communication. It's me saying, "hi there, friends, remind me I exist as more than worry pls".

It's not a mirror, except in the magic sense. It connects me. My wi-fi connection puts a gods-damned girdle around the earth in twenty minutes. And that girdle ties me to you with ribbons made of purest data and that is *magic.*

Because I'm not supposed to feel this way, and reaching out helps me work out how I *want* to feel.

It's not a mirror; it's archaeology. It's a record of my experience for future versions of me to unearth and remember it wasn't all bad. For alternate versions of me to dig up and see how far I've come. It's that long gallery in a country house with all those portraits of the family's ancestors – it's all those dead me's that I carry around.

And, sometimes, yeah, it is a mirror.

It's a mirror that I look into and, for a little while, I can hear the voices of my friends drowning out the voices telling me I'm ugly. Awful. Worthless.

It's a mirror that lets me see myself without *hating* it.

Because I'm not supposed to feel this way and it's really nice to sometimes *not feel this way.*

Because it's not a fair fight – the voices who tell me I'm nothing *never stop*, so how fucking *dare* you tell me the magical thing that lets my friends fight back at any given time is *vanity.*

How dare you tell me I'm not supposed to feel this way.

Librarian

W HEN THE LIBRARIAN came to visit our town, we
were thrilled. No librarian had ever ventured so
far out into the wasteland before and, given how many
books had been torn apart for reasons of kindling and
fanaticism in the bad years, we had been satisfying our
literary needs with John Grisham novels and old Beano
almanacs.

The librarian rode into town upon a horse – no, a
steed – thrown together from old Arthurian romances. It
had been ridden hard and its sides shone with ink sweat
and tales of love, valour and violence. It whinnied and the
sound was of clashing steel and heavy sighs. It was
majestic.

She had clearly come across trouble out in the wastes,
for her armoured cardigan was burnt and ripped, and her
razor-sharp hairpin was wet with blood that dripped from
the tight bun that held up her hair. She adjusted her
glasses as we came into view, the intricate lenses whirring

as they established range, targeting and likely reading preferences.

Some townspeople had tried to deny her entry, afraid of the knowledge she might bring – for the librarians considered all knowledge sacred no matter how dark or vile it might be. But they quieted as she undid the padlock and withdrew the library from her pocket…

It glinted dangerously beneath the desert sun, but she stroked it with her ink and blood-stained fingers and whispered soothing Dewey decimals until it purred. Its purrs sounded like rustling pages and faint screams.

Then it unfolded, a hundred times a hundred times a hundred spines spinning out in a fractal pattern of shelves. They settled around the librarian in a shape that was not-entirely unlike a globe. The order was intricate and hard to discern, seeming to fit together by some strange, organic classification. It looked, perhaps, most like the skeleton of one of the creatures that sometimes crept out of the caves at night.

We were transfixed. The books seemed to call to us. We spent weeks exploring the corners of the structure, not so much reading as inhaling the volumes within.

Then she was gone, headed off further into the interior. Her steed fed on the happy sighs of its readers. Her hairpins sharpened to dangerous points.

I think, by then, we had all fallen a bit in love with her.

Or perhaps just the stories.

The Tree Who Wanted
to be a Girl

ONCE UPON A time there was a tree who wanted to be a girl.

So she always made sure to be the best tree she *could* be, keeping her limbs just the right height for adventurous girls to climb, strong enough to bear their weight and peppered with soft leaves to break their falls. Her spring blossoms always smelt the sweetest and her fruits in the summer hung low, heavy and lush, and if you bit one the juice would run dark down your mouth like delicious, sticky blood.

And in the winter she grew thorns, because you never knew what dodgy buggers would come sniffing around in the winter.

Then one day a man came. He smelt her blossoms in the spring and sighed ever so deeply. He tasted her fruit in the summer and stroked her rough bark in thanks. Then, in winter, she relaxed her thorns to let him in to see her, for she was quite fond of him by then.

And the man brought an axe with him.

When the tree passed back into the earth, she wished on her life's spilled sap to come back as the kind of girl who would never be fooled by the promises of men, no matter how dizzying their words.

She wished for thorns.

But when the earth made her again of its clay, she still wore flowers in her hair and on her skin.

Because she'd be damned if she'd let them take those from her too.

Plant Yourself Like A Tree

"YOUR MAJESTY," THE seneschal's voice was so oily it practically slipped into his ear, "I didn't want to bother you with this, but the knights are having a problem with a woman."

The King paused in the act of putting on his shining armour. They rode to war soon and he needed to make a good impression.

"So?" He flicked a speck of dirt from his perfect breastplate. "Give her a gold coin and tell her to send the brat to the legions when it turns fourteen."

"That was my instinct as well, your majesty," the seneschal wrung his hands, "but it turns out she is not with child."

"What's the problem then?"

"We don't know. She won't say anything. She's just standing there on the drawbridge getting in the way."

The King decided he would see this for himself.

❦

THE KING HAD been shouting at the woman for hours now.

He was red in the face, the wind had stuck his thin hair up in wild spikes, and his gleaming breastplate was covered in flecks of spittle.

He saw the faces of his subjects as they crowded around this peculiar scene. They stared at him with sad, piteous eyes.

"Have her thrown over the side," he spat to his seneschal.

Two knights seized the woman. She simply smiled. They shoved and pulled and huffed and puffed, but her feet were planted firmly in the wood of the drawbridge.

As the knights looked closer, they realised they were *growing* out of the wood.

"Leave off," muttered the King. "I'm going to bed. If she's still there in the morning, cut off her head."

The kingdom held its breath.

COME THE MORNING, there was not a single woman standing on the drawbridge.

Instead, there were six. Their legs sprouted from the splintered cracks in the bridge, growing up into strong, smiling figures.

The King stormed out with a cadre of knights. He was dressed in a nightgown with a little bobbly hat.

He gave a short, inaudible command.

The kingdom watched as the knights blunted their swords on the wooden ladies' necks.

The next day, there were twelve of them.

The next, there were twenty-four.

The King stopped leaving the castle.

The women continued to grow in size and number until a forest of smiling trees surrounded it.

These days, no one remembers the name of the king.

But everyone knows what a woman can do, if she plants herself like a tree and refuses to move.

The Knight and the Dragon

W HEN THE KNIGHT and the Dragon came face-to-face at last they flew towards each other like arrows fired from a bow or comets falling from the sky.

But just before impact, their eyes met and they faltered, each recognising something of themselves in the other.

"From the honour in your eyes I see you are not a dragon, but a knight!" said the Knight. "Come back to court with me."

So the Dragon took human form and joined the Knight as a comrade-in-arms, the Dragon became the scourge of the lists at every tourney, and the two did great deeds together.

But the Dragon felt the constraints of court begin to chafe at her wings, for she was never meant to live in a stone shell.

She said to the Knight: "From the wildness in your eyes I see you are not a knight, but a dragon. Join me in the skies."

And the Knight left her steed behind and climbed up upon the Dragon's back and they spiralled like smoke up to the heavens. The Knight learned the wonders of storms and made lightning her lance and the two of them made everything that lived in the sky their plaything.

But the Knight felt her edges begin to blur in the vast wilds of the sky, for she was never meant to drown in thunder.

So they parted, the Knight a little wilder, and the Dragon a little more honourable, than when they met.

Autopsy

"THE HIGHLIGHT OF my day was licking spatters of adrenal gland off this window," she said, coquettishly.

"I don't think that sounded as coquettish as you hoped it would," I said from behind the bulletproof glass window.

"Oh no. It did," she said, licking her remaining lip with what, once upon a time, had been a tongue.

"Can we just try to keep it professional?" I sighed. Behind the glass, the other dead things shuffled and jostled over the last remaining morsels of dead flesh in the morgue.

"Sorry, Elle, it's hard to think when I'm just *buzzing* like this. We don't often get real food. It is a veritable corpse party up in here," she said, swiping another ghoul into the wall with her wicked talons. For a moment, her eyes filled up with blood and she seemed like she was lost. Then she shook her head and blinked until her eyes went grey again. "I'm sorry… what was I saying?"

"Gill–" I swallowed her name before I could finish saying it. It was bitter. "Could you just tell me what you found out about the body?"

"Which body? There's hella bodies down here."

"The one you ate. You still have… gobbets on your face."

I hated coming down here, but this was the closest thing we had to an autopsy these days.

"Yeah, and gobbets are all I got. The flock down here are greedy during a feeding frenzy. Sure you don't want to come in here and give me a snack?"

"Not really."

"Aw." She tried to wink. Once upon a time, her wink had been the thing that made me sure. That always got the butterflies in a tizzy in my stomach. It no longer had that effect on me. "You used to like it when I bit you."

I tried my best to blank out the memory of whisky, teeth and gasped breath that sprang to mind. I didn't especially like remembering those days, back when we were both studying medicine and had barely even heard words like "ghoul" or "hellfire".

"I'm asking you nicely," I said, my left hand twitching as it hovered over the taser strapped to my hip, "but I *need* you to cooperate here. People are starting to talk. Ugly words. 'Danger'. 'Monster'. If I'm gonna keep you here, I need to show them you have *value*."

"I…" She looked at me and concentrated very hard. I

could see the dark veins standing out in her eyes. "…you don't think I have value."

"Please. Focus. I have a dead body here."

"You have more than one."

I would not have thought before that a walking corpse could look forlorn.

"Just. Be a *person*." I used to use that line on her back when she was alive and being difficult. I nearly choked on the words this time. "Just for a minute. Then I can make sure you get to stay."

She cocked her head at me, her neck cracking as she did so. For a moment I wasn't sure if she was looking at me like an ex or like a meal. I wasn't sure which was worse.

"Be a person, she says." Her voice is very quiet, croaking in the ruin of her throat. "But what you *need* is the ghoul with her freakish tastebuds."

I held her gaze.

"Please."

She bared her rotting teeth. For a moment, I thought I'd lost her. Then she reached into her mouth and took a small morsel of flesh from a crack between one tooth.

"Okay," she said, speaking carefully and falteringly, struggling to make sense of the words "here's what you've got: cause of death was cardiac arrest brought about by a massive dose of some kind of intoxicant. It tasted weird."

She paused for a minute, there was a sound not unlike a laugh that rumbled in her throat.

"Sheriff, you've got yourself a murder."

I turned away without another word. Something burned in my chest.

On my way back up through the hospital, I took a second to buff the tacky plastic badge pinned to my chest.

I really hated this job sometimes.

The ballad of Anastasia Cathy Jane Isabella Bella Stella Blanche Katherina Steele

I'm plain and clumsy
My hair is mousy brown
My eyes are muddy
Or maybe violet
I can never remember
Maybe in this story they're green.
I like it when they're green.
My hair's a mess
Brushes would get lost in there
My hair's a wild wilderness
My hair's got tangles that could kill a man
I hate my hair
Only he would call me beautiful
Only he calls me beautiful

But I'm plain and clumsy
So it must mean he loves me.
At least, he says he loves me.
So that must be it.
He loves me even though I'm clumsy
And like books more than people
Even though I'm all sarcastic and talk back
That's why I always have bruises.
Because I'm clumsy
And don't know how to walk in heels.
But he sees through the bruises
And the hair
And my plain-ness.
He sees me.
His eyes are wide
His eyes are hungry
For me.
He makes my heart flutter.
That's a *good thing*.
His name is Christian
Or Edward, or Heathcliff or maybe Rochester at a push.
Probably not Darcy.
His name doesn't matter.
In every story, it's always him.
His skin is cold against mine
Like he's dead or rain-soaked
Or emotionally distant
It's definitely not fear.

I'm not afraid.

He told me he was dangerous

He told me.

He told me because he cares.

Because he doesn't want to hurt me.

Because he could never hurt me.

He would only ever let *me* get close to him

Because he's dangerous

But he cares so much

He can't *not* see me.

He keeps me close to him because he loves me.

Because the world is dangerous.

Because he loves me.

We're naked now.

He's ripped off my clothes

He's that wild.

He wants me that much

And we're naked now.

He's the first man to see me naked.

He's the first man to see me.

It hurts, but that's a *good thing*.

My skin is tingling

My skin is alive with goosebumps

My skin is electricity

This is like static, stormy electricity

That's what it's like.

My skin's not crawling.

It hurts because it should

Because I like it.

It's sexy

It must be

He loves me

They wrote him to love me

They made him out of words and dreams and unspeakable
    desires

So he would *love* me

He was made for it

That's what he says, at least.

I'm trembling with want.

Or at the very least

I'm trembling.

The Girl With The Switch

ONCE UPON A time, there was a little girl who could turn off her feelings.

The switch had grown out of her neck when she was young and she had been most surprised when she flipped it for the first time and found herself wrapped in a pleasant void.

At first she would use it sparingly, when she realised her toddler tantrums were getting her nowhere and the rage became bothersome. Or in the adolescent period when she had been crying for days and was just *so* tired.

In her teen years, she would use it to take a break from particularly distracting crushes so she could actually get some work done. Sometimes she would flick it on to better endure the last five minutes of the phone call with her best friend who was also her worst enemy.

When she was grown and had learned more about the world, she discovered that she had *opinions* about said world's state. This was when the switch came into its own, for she soon discovered those opinions were far more palatable for those around her when she was able to express them with as little expression as possible.

She discovered work went much more agreeably, too, if she was able to take interruptions, implied insults and incompetent imperatives with placid acceptance. Then she would flick the switch back on and resume the work of being relentlessly *good* at things.

She found romance so much easier to navigate when she was incapable of heartbreak or disappointment.

Then, one day, she flipped the switch to turn her feelings back on and she thought that the switch must have been broken for she felt no difference.

Using a complex system of mirrors and scalpels, she investigated the space behind the switch and saw her feelings there. They had curled up into a dry, withered ball, with fragile, petrified strands reaching out from their cracked mass.

It looked for all the world like the husk of a starved plant.

She shrugged and sewed herself back up.

Things went much smoother for her from that day onwards.

The Devil Wears Body Armour

S HE MISSED HER costume.

The smart shirt collar dug into her neck (but was necessary to hide the bruises), and its cotton polyester felt like paper compared to her usual pinstripe armours.

She hated this undercover crap.

She didn't mind danger, that was part of the job, but she preferred to face it head on. Like, literally headbutt it. Headbutting featured a lot in her dreams these days.

Meanwhile, she was spending her days interviewing for PA jobs, trying to infiltrate companies with suspected supervillainous connections. That day she was interviewing for a fashion company (a front for the mob), where the chairman was rumoured to be a battleaxe of a woman with a penchant for clumsy, passive co-eds with messy hair.

It was like The Devil Wears 50 Fucking Shades of Grey Prada up in here.

And she kept reaching for her utility belt and finding

it wasn't there.

Still, she'd managed to get away with sewing a surprising number of pockets into her office outfit.

Pockets were good.

They were an urban camo utility belt.

An armour made of zips, crevices and bits of string.

They stopped her feeling quite so naked.

Plus, her earrings were totally phosphorous grenades and that took some of the edge off, too.

Well Emo

S HE WAS WAITING for him in the alley's mouth, a stake held casually in one hand and murder in her eyes.

"So, what kind of vampire are you?"

"I don't understand the question."

"Like, are you proper sparkly or are you well goth? Cos, mate, either way you're getting dusted, but if you're the sparkly kind I'll save some 'cos the glittery ashes are well glam."

He smiled and let himself unfold, the shadows unfurling around him until he seemed little more than a black hole draped around sharp teeth.

"My dear, I am the kind of vampire who has lived for centuries. I have seen the rise and fall of empires. I have drunk both with and from philosophers, kings and paupers. I have lived for so long that your lives seem to pass me by in a blur, each of you a single frame of a far longer film reel – each life supremely brief and pointless and more beautiful for that. I have worn midnight like a lover across my skin and stared down the rising sun until it retreated from me."

He took a deep breath, his nebulous form puffing out like a venomous thing. It was pure affectation; he had long ago ceased the habit of respiration.

"Bruv, you are *well* emo." She holstered the stake. "Fancy a coffee?"

"I do not drink ... coffee."

He paused for a second.

"I could murder a tea, though."

Cryptic

AFTER THE OCCUPATION, the princess was confined to the palace.

Once a month she'd be taken on a walk around the city, heavily guarded of course, to show the people that she still lived. It also served, of course, as a reminder of what the potential insurgents stood to lose if they made trouble. The princess did her best to wave and smile and give the people what encouragement she could.

The rest of the time, her life was spent in musty rooms and dusty towers. She filled most of her days scouring the castle for materials which she would sew into more and more elaborate outfits, which she would show off when she was allowed outside.

Indeed, the public loved their princess and her dresses so much they'd often sketch or paint them along the route and pass the images on so that all could see the princess at least was well.

This pleased the occupiers for two reasons. First: it

kept the princess out of trouble. Second: it gave them a reason to sneer. They did love a good sneer.

"What a vain creature she is!" they would remark.

"Doesn't even care we murdered her brothers so long as she gets enough satin to make her little dresses!" they squawked.

This was unfair, of course. For to call her creations "little dresses" was to call the Mona Lisa "a picture of a lady with sort of a weird smile". Her dresses were gravity-defying wonders of lace and pearl. They were thunderstorms captured in velvet and waterfalls summoned in silk. She was a wizard with silk.

Still, she bore their mockery with a tight smile and careful deference.

"Please, good sirs, my home, my people and my city now belong to you. Let me keep, at least, this one last joy."

And they sneered and they crowed most unpleasantly, but they let her keep her sewing room.

Of course, they would have known their mockery to be doubly unfair had they realised the true purpose of the princess's elaborate designs. For hidden in the intricate embroidery across her gowns, jackets and fans, the princess had encoded secret (and very detailed) messages. When she would go on her monthly walk, the city's loyalists would line the route, sketching down the patterns to decode later.

Thus did the princess transmit all the occupiers' secrets (unearthed while supposedly 'searching the castle for old fabrics') to the city and thus did she build her resistance.

On the day the revolution finally came, she girded herself in armour of thick spider silk and whale bone. She cut a fine figure with a lacy handkerchief in her top pocket and a razor sharp knitting needle keeping her hair up.

As she waltzed through the castle to open the door for her army, the Usurper King tried to stop her and she simply unfolded her handkerchief and showed it to him.

Upon seeing the impossible arcane pattern emblazoned across it, he fell to the floor with blood streaming from his eyes.

She always had been a wizard with silk.

The Sculptor, The Sorcerer and the Golem

W HEN THE SCULPTOR was young, the way the clay danced beneath her fingers made her the darling of the court.

Her creations were wonders, things of perfect and primal beauty – at once both intricate and raw. It was said that to own one of her artworks was to know the creator.

That was how she first caught the attention of The Sorcerer. For in her art he saw a reflection of his own raw magic, and became determined to know her heart.

They were very good at being very bad for each other, clashing furiously and making up equally furiously. Both their love and their hate had a kind of intense, tidal beauty to it.

When they finally broke from each other, they did so violently, leaving jagged, uneven edges that never quite healed cleanly.

That was when The Sorcerer laid a curse upon the sculptor.

"I told myself I would know your heart, my love," he said in the ancient language of creation, "and so I shall. For if you do not surrender your still-beating heart to me in precisely a year's time, then the earth itself shall rise and shatter this land."

But the sculptor was clever. Determined to find a way around the sorcerer's curse, she began to construct a golem.

Now, golems were fairly commonplace in their land and were considered, as a rule, to be intelligent and reliable tools. It was fairly ordinary for their masters to create them with functioning brains. It was unheard of, however, for them to be given working *hearts*.

But that is what the sculptor did. She carefully moulded it from the clay taken from near a volcano, so it would have the necessary fire to spark its feelings. And when she baked it, she made sure it was strong enough to contain rage, but not so brittle as to shatter from tragedy.

When the baby golem awoke she fed it on her own tears until it grew strong. Then, when it was old enough, she took it to court to find adventure so its heart would grow hardy. And the golem made sure it used its powerful limbs to protect the sculptor's squishy flesh from the various monsters they faced.

She introduced it to the court's gentlemen and ladies so it might know heartbreak and grow from it.

She told it the story of her life in all its many tragedies and triumphs – all except, that is, the story of her eventual curse.

Before she knew it, a year had passed. She took the golem to meet The Sorcerer.

"What is this?" he cried. "You expect to wriggle out of your curse by force?"

"No," she said. "I had thought to make a beating heart from clay that I could give in place of my own."

She looked at the golem's wide furnace eyes.

"But I find I cannot bring myself to do that to my own creation."

And she took out a dagger and held it to her chest.

"Stop!" said the golem. "Your flesh is very squishy and you will not survive. Let me do what I was made for and give my heart instead."

"I am sorry," she replied. "There are some things I have to do for myself. Squishy flesh and all. I have taught you the workings of the clay and the kiln, my beloved creation. I am content to let you continue my work."

And she plunged the dagger into her chest as The Sorcerer laughed.

...

When she woke, she was surprised to feel the steady, warm beat of a heart in her chest.

She looked down to see the gaping wound had been plugged with a fresh layer of clay.

She looked up to see the golem standing over her and

she reached for it immediately, wrapping her arms as far as she could around its mountain of a chest. Her own chest ached fiercely and she was greatly surprised to find that it felt whole – albeit her skin felt somewhat strange and cold. She looked around her; they were in her workshop and the golem's hands were stained with clay and blood.

She took a better look at the golem. Beneath her embrace, there was a gaping hole in its chest.

"You didn't…" she said, weakly.

"You needed it more than me," it said.

"Besides," it pointed to the kiln, "my new heart is nearly ready."

Lightness of Being

ANGELICA USED TO have a problem with her heart.
It wasn't a murmur or tremor or anything like that; instead, her heart was simply far too light.

It was wonderful for her disposition – the weight of the world simply fell away from her as she floated and bounced her way around existence.

Then she *really* started to float, pulled up by her chest as if it were full of hydrogen that longed to return to the sky.

She enjoyed the feeling of flight immensely – and found enormous joy to be discovered from exploring the world from amongst the clouds. Something about the angle of approaching life from above was deeply pleasing, for she had never been the tallest of people.

But, after a while, she began to lose touch with her still-earthbound friends. It is, after all, difficult to relate to people when you only see them from above. Swooping down, she asked them how they could be so heavy of heart as to be trapped in the dirt.

"We are not heavy of heart," they said, "our hearts would be as light as yours if only we were not tied down so."

And it was not until Angelica looked closely that she saw the translucent wires that held them, tying them in great and complex tangles. And at the centre of those tangles were a writhing mass of ghosts – hateful creatures who span the strands of the wires together. Worse still, she noticed, was that some of the wires were barbed…

Angelica's heart became heavy for the first time as she flew into a rage and the hydrogen in her chest erupted. Filled with fire, she tried to burn through the wires that held her friends.

"It is not that easy", they told her, as the wraiths' pale hands blurred to repair the damage. "These chains were forged over centuries by these ghosts when they were alive. And the knots are so tight it is hard for even us to see how they fit together. If we are to be free to fly, we must work our way through back to the source. For there can be no true flight without freedom."

Angelica nodded and thought for a while.

Then she seized a handful of the wires, felt the barbs bite into her fingers, and heaved upwards with all her might.

The others relaxed for a second, for just a second, as she took the strain they'd borne so long. Then her strength gave out and the weight settled on their shoulders – albeit, slightly lighter than it was before.

Angelica still flew slightly higher than most of her friends, but she bore what she could of their weight. And they used the slack to make headway at the knots that held them.

Thusly, together, did they slowly unravel the ties of history – and together they all dreamed of flight.

Changed

ONCE UPON THERE was a little boy who lived in a faraway village in the woods.

One day he went into the woods.

He was never seen again.

No one had much cared for him anyway.

Several years later a woman emerged from nowhere, wearing a sea serpent as her only clothing.

The kingdom fell.

No one had much cared for it anyway.

Lost

WHEN THE DROWNED Man first met the Sea Witch, they were both lost.

She, metaphorically, for the King of the Undersea had just exiled her from the deep trench for daring to suggest totalitarian monarchy was not the most modern arrangement. The shallow waters with their strange, contrary currents felt like a maze. And her rage hemmed her in on all sides.

He, literally, for the ship on which he travelled had been caught in the tempest thrown up by the King's wrath and shook to flotsam. He had battled his way through the surf that claimed his friends, his crew and his shoes. The stones of this strange, storm-swept beach were like knives on his feet.

They both cried out in despair at the same time.

"Jinx," said the Sea Witch, claiming her first voice.

In exchange, she heard his silent pleas for direction and furnished him with a map.

He followed it to many strange places. Coastal caves lit by glowing algae. Ships wrecked on sharp rocks, containing shifting treasures he could neither carry nor understand. A castle raised high on a craggy tower in the middle of a perfectly calm, dead sea.

From each of these places, he brought back a trinket. Three shards of coral. An old, barnacle-encrusted stick. A conch filled with sticky black ink.

In the meantime, the Sea Witch scoured the ocean beds for what he had lost.

She fought off the merpeople who guarded the King's borders, flinging stinging curses and bloody kisses at them 'til they surrendered their salvage.

She made a deal with the reaper of the deep, who was all teeth and despair. They sealed their pact in blood and poetry woven through the song of passing whales.

She let Leviathan swallow her and burst through his skin, covered in ichor and holding a pair of old boots.

When the Drowned Man and the Sea Witch met once more on the shore, he gave the trinkets to her and she slotted the coral into the stick to make a trident, then soaked the points in kraken ink.

Behind her sailed a broken ship, bound together with seaweed and crewed by the man's drowned fellows. Their skin was pale and covered in limpets and spiked urchins.

She returned to him his boots and his voice.

They rode the wrecked ship down into the trench, storming the Undersea with their crew of storm-dead sailors.

They screamed with rage as they plunged the trident into the King's black heart.

Later, when the tumult had died down, they met on the shore once more.

"Let's be friends," he said. "And build a world that doesn't need *anyone* to rule it."

"Yes, let's," she replied.

Scheherazade

L ET'S TALK ABOUT Scheherazade.

Let's talk about her telling a story every night. One that hung in the air, heavy with spice and magic.

Let's talk about her entrancing the king so completely; her words of enchantment had the precise worth of a life.

Or we could look at it another way.

Imagine she had a small vial, made of pure and unbreakable crystal. And in this vial swirled a storm cloud. And that cloud was really nanites.

And every night, she poured a wisp of the smoke into his ear. And the robots crawled inside him and rearranged him from within.

And every morning, he woke up and she had made him a slightly different person.

A more merciful person.

And by the time she told her 1001st tale, not a mote of the man she'd met on the first night remained.

Of course, she did not have these things.

But this is still what her stories did. The king was not enchanted, but as every story changed him a little bit, he was *transfigured*.

It is what happens whenever we hear a story.

It is happening to you now.

Red

ONCE UPON A time there was a little girl who had a red hood that she loved very much. She had been given it by her grandmother, who she also loved very much (but not as much as the hood).

One day she took a basket of treats through the woods to where her grandmother lived. Little did she know that her beloved gran, grown fearful that she was not long for this world, had made a blood pact with a local monster (who took the form of a wolf). The deal was this: Granny would deliver her kids and grandkids to the wolf monster for devouring and the monster would make granny young again.

Long story short: there were some very big teeth and the girl got ate.

(Also, the wolf stole her red hood, which *really* narked her off).

Then a woodcutter also got ate (but he was just collateral damage).

And as the woodcutter was slowly dissolved in the wolf's stomach, the little girl fumed. The anger rolled off her in waves, repelling the wolf monster's attempts to digest her.

She sat there in his stomach for a long time, sustained by her rage, steam rising from her skin as she got angrier and angrier. She was there for years, for decades, her fury keeping her ever young. The monster could feel her squatting whole inside him, cramping up his insides and churning bile.

In time, her heat grew until the hairs on her arms became kindling and she sparked into flame. The monster bellowed as the fires licked his innards, he coughed and swallowed and tried to keep her down, but eventually – in one agonising belch – he vomited her up.

She blazed. He shrank away, but her brilliance blinded his big eyes. The roar of flames filled his big ears. She reached for him, part girl part wildfire, and the inferno melted his big teeth.

She left him there, a burnt husk of fur and fear.

Then she went to see her grandmother.

The girl found her in her cottage, placing the red hood across her too-young skin, preparing to go out on the town.

Seeing her granddaughter wreathed in fire, she cowered and pleaded. She threw off the red hood and just screamed, "Take it! Don't hurt me, just take it."

And the girl took the hood in her hand and it burnt

right up. The cinders danced in front of her eyes and she flicked out her tongue to taste the ash.

"When you are old again," the girl said in a hiss like an extinguished candle, "think on your aches and pains and remember me."

And she left. Her grandmother lay on the floor, gasping breaths through her perfect chest and stared into the advancing years.

The girl walked across the unfamiliar town where her woods had used to be and the people gasped in fear and wonder.

The fire clung to her like a cloak.

Hungry

"**F**REEDOM FIGHTER? HA!" She flicks out her lighter as if to punctuate the laugh and lights a cigarette. I glance at the 'no smoking' sign, but say nothing. Neither does anyone else.

"If it weren't for the fact that we won, you would be calling us terrorists... besides, it wasn't freedom that we fought for."

She sucks down smoke and belches it out like a cannon.

"Then what?" I'm conscious that my beer is sitting untouched by my dictaphone, while she has nearly finished hers.

"Freedom. Justice. Revolution. Such big words." She taps out her ash onto the floor. "Who can see these things from so close?"

I'm not sure if you can call what passes across her face a smile. For just a moment, her skin becomes a landscape – her mouth a deep, curved ravine.

"Freedom is ninety percent hindsight. You wake up one day, years later, and think '*Huh. We're... free? Is that what this is? Did... did we do this? Shit*'."

She laughs again and her battle scars seem flesh once more.

"At the time, we were just fighting because we were hungry."

She downs her beer and another is already on the table.

"Which, I suppose, might be one of the edges of freedom."

Star-Crossed

T HE FIRST TIME she lost herself in a book was Romeo and Juliet.

The first time, that is, in more than a metaphorical sense. For the words twisted and the story squirmed before her eyes and the shadows in her imagination flickered into life.

She landed in the fight scene. Romeo was riddling Tybalt with platitudes, trying to avoid crossing swords with his secret kinsman. Meanwhile, Mercutio peppered the air with verbal sparks and the scene was hot with the fire of scorched egos.

There was something hyper-real about them. The perfect skin, unblemished like fresh parchment. The voices echoing across the cobbled streets, perfectly enunciated and seeming to come from everywhere and nowhere. The flush a perfect rose in their cheeks.

Then the splash of red, as Tybalt's blade burst the bubble of blood as it slid through Romeo's throat.

The terror that this *wasn't how it was supposed to go*.

Mercutio, vengeful, careless and fabulous, flying through the air in a flash of steel and spitting rage.

The dizzy swagger to his step, even as he swayed from a wound deep as a well and wide as a barn door.

Then Romeo's sword was in her hand, a barb on her lips and, before she knew what was happening, Tybalt's heartblood embraced her blade and palms.

She wandered through the banishment dazed.

But she just about remembered enough of who she was to refrain from swallowing the fateful draught and see the breath flow back into Juliet's surprisingly powerful lungs.

Their introduction was an awkward one, but Juliet was thrilled by the idea they should flee the city with her disguised as a man.

The story ended happily, far from Verona.

And, eventually, she woke from the tale like a dream – the taste of ink and Juliet's kisses on her lips.

Why Why Why

AFTER SHE'D CUT off his hair, Delilah wove it into a bracelet and spent the next few years winning feats of strength and fighting crime and all sorts.

Feeling sorry for him, she agreed to lend Samson his hair one last time.

As she picked the bracelet out of the rubble, she took a second to smile and approve of her own life choices.

The Girl Who Punched The Sky

OR AS LONG as she could remember, she had always hated the sky.

She despised the way it loomed over her.

The way it spat rain on her.

She hated the colours blue and grey with equal intensity.

She resented the way it took credit for the stars and moon (the sun could go suck a supernova for all she cared).

She could just about tolerate snow, and had been known to skip blithely through blizzards, muttering things like "I hope you freeze to death you overbearing, cloudy bastard", much to the consternation of the clouds of ice elementals that danced around her and bounced off her skin.

Mainly, she hated the sky for the way it made her feel.

In the dim recesses of her DNA, coiled at the core of her, was a remembrance of flight. Of giddy swoops and soarings through the cool glitter of clouds. Of tying jetstream strings around the globe.

But her antecedents had fallen long ago and she had no wings, just a lingering sense of absence.

That, and a talent for machines.

The engines that sprung up around her could only be described as infernal. A forest of belching flame and crackling static.

In her early experiments she had thrown lightning upwards, lancing the heavens with light and laughing as the taste of ozone sparked off her teeth.

The sky had just laid there and taken it.

But she had always had bigger plans. And now, as she sped upwards through the air with hellfire licking at her feet (and the screams of the demons she'd bound into her rocket boots tearing through the wind), she finally looked at the sky with a smile on her face.

Her hair flared wild in a halo of writhing electric incubi.

Her silver-covered fist sang the song of atoms.

Cracks spread across the sky's impassive face, revealing a glimpse of the welcoming void behind it.

Red rain fell upon the land.

She had bloodied the sky's nose and everything had changed.

Deus Ex

H EPHAESTUS 4 WAS colloquially known as The Galaxy's Junkyard.

Once a planet renowned for its construction industry, new nano-based technologies had rendered its city-wide factories obsolete and now its colossal shipyards lay rusting beneath its three suns.

And, over time, even the satellites and space stations that orbited the planet fell and crashed to earth in great blazing trails of debris. Thus the defunct industrial zones became scrap heaps.

Those who were left on the surface and unable to afford passage off-world scraped a living by salvaging parts and trading them with the few junk merchants who still visited. But the price of passage was steep and few could ever pull together the funds – and none were ever sure how far the junkers could be trusted to provide safe transport…

To pass the time between salvage runs, the

Haphaestians developed games and sports using whatever could be found. By far the most popular of these was Battle Skating, a game in which two teams dressed in scrap armour and, wielding empty fuel rods as swords, would joust at each other with mechanical wheels strapped to their feet.

The rules were many and complicated (with a tendency to evolve as the game went on), so those who could master the game were celebrated as the kings and queens of their junk piles. It's widely accepted that the greatest known player was Deus Ex Thrashina, a fearsome woman and ace mechanic who ruled the tracks with lightning speed.

But Thrashina, despite her success on the tracks, always had one eye to the heavens and spent *hours* tinkering on some secret project in her workshop.

It finally became clear what she was working on at the end of one season's championship game. Having led her team to a stunning victory, the cheer of the crowd still ringing in her custom-made helmet, her celebration lap became faster and faster until the crowd were dizzied keeping up with her. Just as it seemed she must slow down or lose control, she sped up a ramp and took off into the sky with two rocket jets billowing flame from beneath her boots.

As her armour closed and became airtight around her, she burned a trail high into the atmosphere.

Most believe she must have burned up making the

escape through the atmosphere, but there are still some who remain certain she made it through and that, even now, she rides through the cosmos on skates of flame...

Systems Failure

W HEN THE SHIP'S core began to lose integrity and
the power spikes arced so fiercely they left the air
scarred, she moved quickly to save what she could.

She had the hull made into a rather fetching jacket.

The thrusters became a pair of stylishly badass boots
with hidden rockets.

The weapons array was hidden inside a rather dashing
cane (totes pimp).

The core itself was trickiest. She slowly untangled the
coiled, sparking energies and, grasping them firmly
between her clawed fingers, she tenderly caressed the
stormy circuitry to calmness.

She took the ends of the quantum relays and carefully
threaded them through her skin, feeling them buck
beneath her cells as they settled into place.

For a moment they flared across her pale form, a
thousand glowing subcutaneous snakes, writhing like
Medusa at a rave. Then the camouflage circuit kicked in

and they settled into static monochrome.

People often commented on the incredibly life-like quality of the dragon tattoo that spread across her. Only occasionally, in times of great emotion, did the power spike and crackle sharply off her skin, betraying the fact that she was at least part starship.

Second Star on the Left

"Second star on the left," he said
But the sky was so full of stars
And I've always been dyspraxic
(he didn't understand the word)
I carried straight on 'til morning
I carried on longer still
I sank my teeth into my happy thoughts
And flew far beyond the stars.
I learnt to sail using Pyxis
I learnt to hunt from Orion
I lost my hand to a crocked star gone nova
I replaced it with a grappling hook.
I made a map of the heavens
And freed Neverland
By stealing the Pan's shadow
To force him to follow me
On an awfully big adventure
Across nebulas beyond Neverland.
I am the girl the Lost Boys lost
But you can call me Captain Wendy –

Acknowledgements

This is really happening isn't it? All these little stories I wrote to try and impress my friends are all snuggled up here together. Gosh. How did this happen? Well, I suppose the first people to blame (after all, blame is just 'credit' by another name) are all the folks who liked and shared these stories when I put them online. I'm an insecure creature at heart, so your encouragement is what kept me writing and posting and improving. Specifically, my first thanks go to Kaida, who was the first person to tell me that not only did they enjoy my writing but that it helped them. I doubt I would have stuck with it if it weren't for knowing that their grey days were brightened by these bizarre little fragments.

Some might think it a little odd for a man to choose to put together a collection on the theme of heroines. And I probably wouldn't have been comfortable doing so if it weren't for the real life heroines who are at the heart of these stories. First and foremost amongst those are my loves: Dana, Jenna, Miranda, Becca and Katie, there are bits of each of you in these pages. Also featured, in no particular order, are the following ladies and entities of mysterious and indistinct gender: Alex D, Ara, Claire S, Lucy, Haplocke, Becka, Sarah, Olwen, Hel, Pam, Lilith, Spell, Claire T, Clare, Sam, Jocelyn, Penn, Alex C. There are many more people that I pretentiously think of as my 'muses' and I adore you all.

Thanks especially again to Lucy Ayrton, my own personal heroine for the last 13 years. Thanks for introducing me to the world of slam poetry, which taught me the art of telling a story in 3 minutes. Big thanks too to Steve Larkin, Tina Sederholm and Neil Spokes; as part of Hammer & Tongue, and as individuals and writers of the highest calibre, I have learned so much and come such a long way thanks to you wonderfully poetic folk.

Big thanks to my parents, who filled my childhood with stories and who showed such indulgence for a child who was always running around having adventures in his own head. Thank you for your patience in realising I was never going to stop playing in those worlds. I'm not sorry ;)

Oh wow, and Sara. The amazing Sara-Jayne Slack. Thank you for taking a chance on my little stories and for helping me work out the theme of this book. Thanks, also, for the patience you showed me in editing and the fantastic collaborative process that was choosing and ordering these tales, and uncanny ability to know exactly what the book needs. Inspired Quill is a fabulous creation – I'm very happy to call it home.

And oh my wow, have y'all seen the cover? Venetia Jackson exceeded my wildest dreams. That cover is so brilliantly badass.

Finally, of course, thank you for reading. The heroines contained in this book mean a very great deal to me; contained within them are the people who inspired me and the lessons they have taught me. I hope you enjoyed meeting them as much as I did.

About the Author

James is an inveterate scribbler of poetry and prose who can most reliably be found writing weird little stories online, on a stage somewhere, doing something that can only be described as 'proclaiming'.

As a poet, he's won multiple slams, performed up and down the UK (mainly down) and written two full-length spoken word theatre shows (*50 Shades of Webster* and *Poor Life Choices*) that he's performed at various festivals and even one sci-fi convention.

When not performing, he's had poetry published in a couple of anthologies, but most often publishes microfiction and flash fiction on his tumblr, Strange Little Stories.

James likes his stories the same way he likes his friends/partners: somewhat surprising, perfectly formed and weird as hell.

Oh, and he lives in Oxford, UK. In case any of you were interested.

Find the author via his website:
strangelittlestories.tumblr.com

Or tweet at him:
@websterpoet